P9-BZW-164

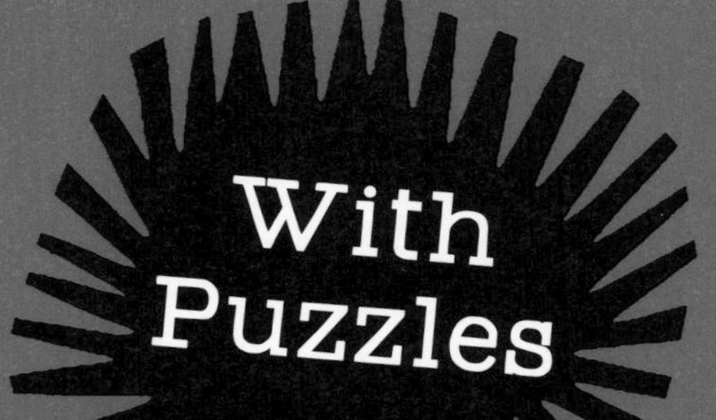


# A Magical Adventure

Illustrations by
Marianna Oklejak

# Once upon a time

there were two brothers,

Jan and Adam.

Their parents had died long ago,

and they had no other family.

It was just the two of them.

After many years their money

ran out, and the brothers began

to quarrel and blame each other

for their troubles.

Finally, they decided to leave their home and seek their fortunes elsewhere.

Find each brother
a piece of bread for
the journey.

6

They soon came to a field filled with birds.

*Find two birds that look the same.*

7

The birds offered help in exchange for a meal.

*Find a snail for each bird.*

9

The birds told Jan and Adam to follow the path until they came to a house where two fairies lived.

Jan tapped on the first window. He didn't want to travel with his brother any longer.

10

Turn to page 12 to see what happened next.

Spot 10 differences between the windows.

Adam tapped on the second window. *He* didn't want to travel with *his* brother any longer.

Turn to page 32 to see what happened next.

The fairy gave Jan a magic ring, so he could see in the dark.

*Find the magic ring; it looks different from all the others.*

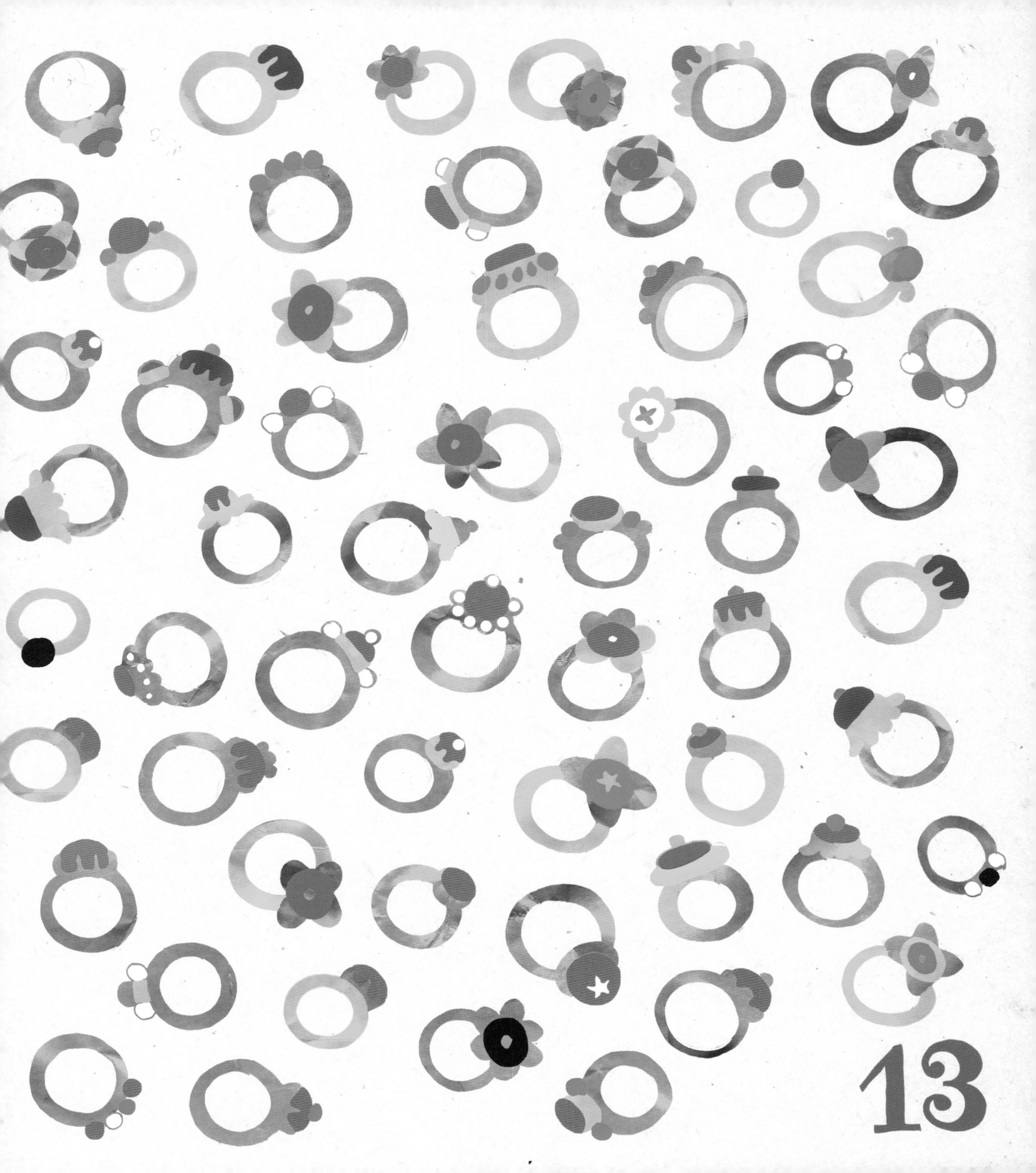
13

14
But the rest of the journey was up to him.
Which path should Jan follow?
Left or right?

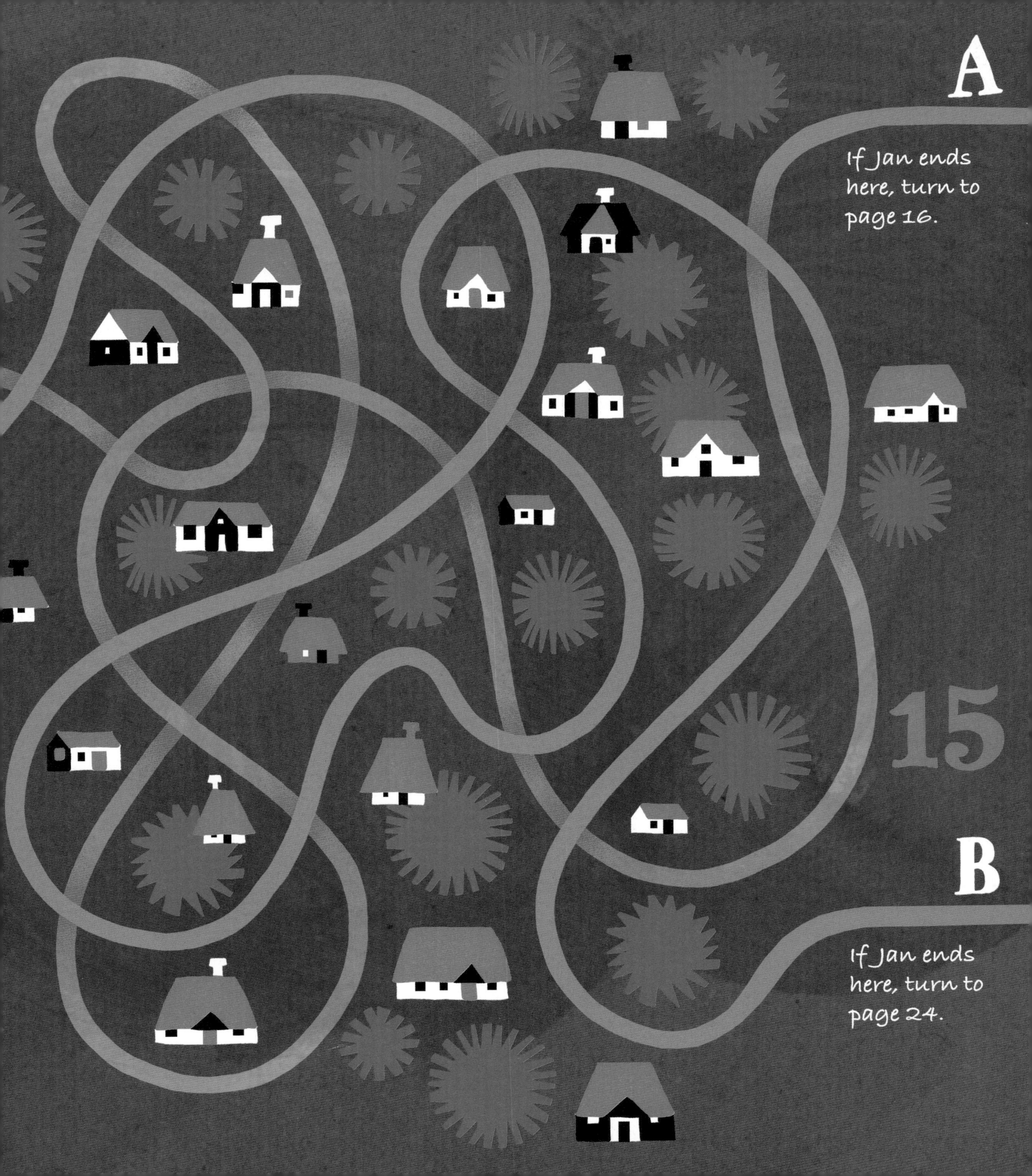
A
If Jan ends here, turn to page 16.
B
If Jan ends here, turn to page 24.

Jan followed the path to a forest. It was dark, and Jan stopped to help a rabbit who was hungry and had lost his way.



*Find 10 mushrooms for the rabbit.*

# 18

Farther into the forest, Jan heard birds singing, wolves howling . . .

*Spot three other animals hiding in the trees.*

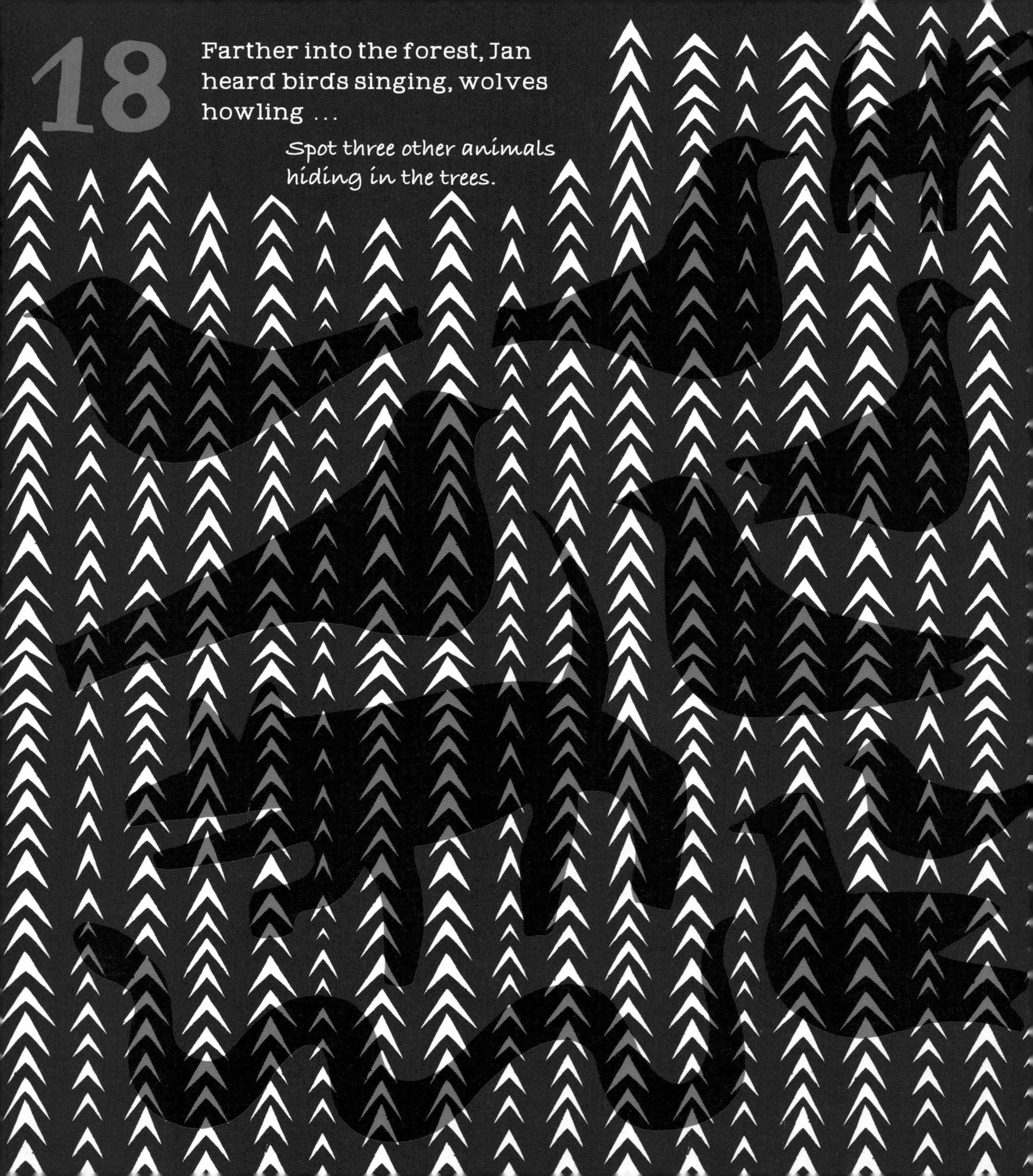

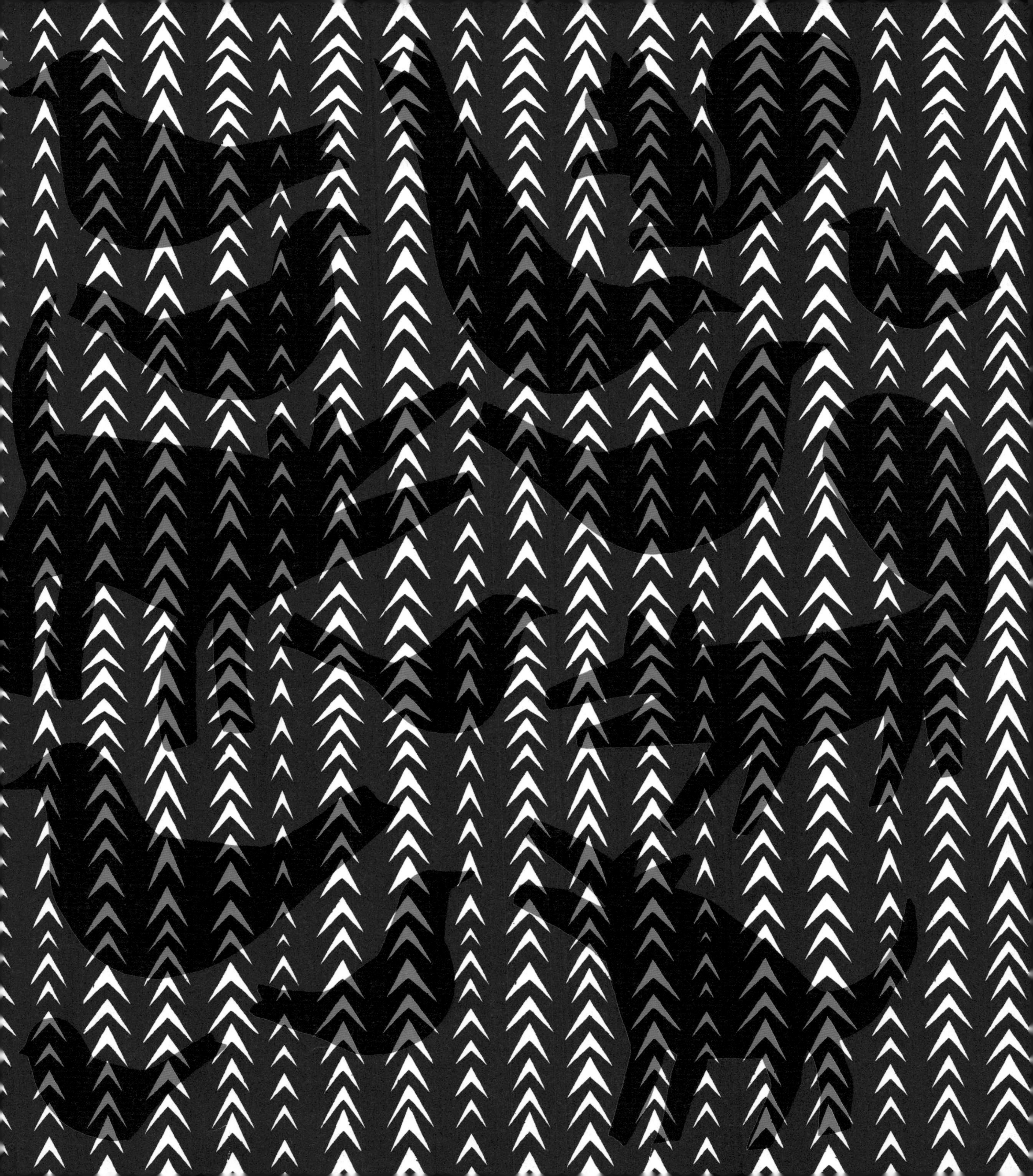

. . . and an ogre, calling to him, offering gold and jewels. All Jan had to do, the ogre said, was to wait until midnight and pick a fern blossom.

*How many snakes are hiding in the grass?*

Then, Jan would be richer than he'd ever dreamed.

*Find the blossom (look carefully!), then turn to page 54.*

24

# 25

Jan followed the path to a field, and disturbed a flock of doves. A falcon watched hungrily.

*Find the falcon, and chase it away.*

Then Jan came upon a magnificent deer next to the river. Jan stopped to help him.

*Spot 5 ticks and 1 flea bothering the deer.*

Jan crossed the river and entered a beautiful garden. He had to take care. An evil witch and strong magic protected the garden from intruders.

28

Find a fly
in the garden.

30

Jan didn't know about the magic. He picked a rose . . . and turned into a peacock!

*Jan the peacock still has the magic ring.*
*Find it and turn to page 44.*

The fairy gave Adam a gold key, but said the rest of the journey was up to him.

*Find the key that looks different than all the others.*

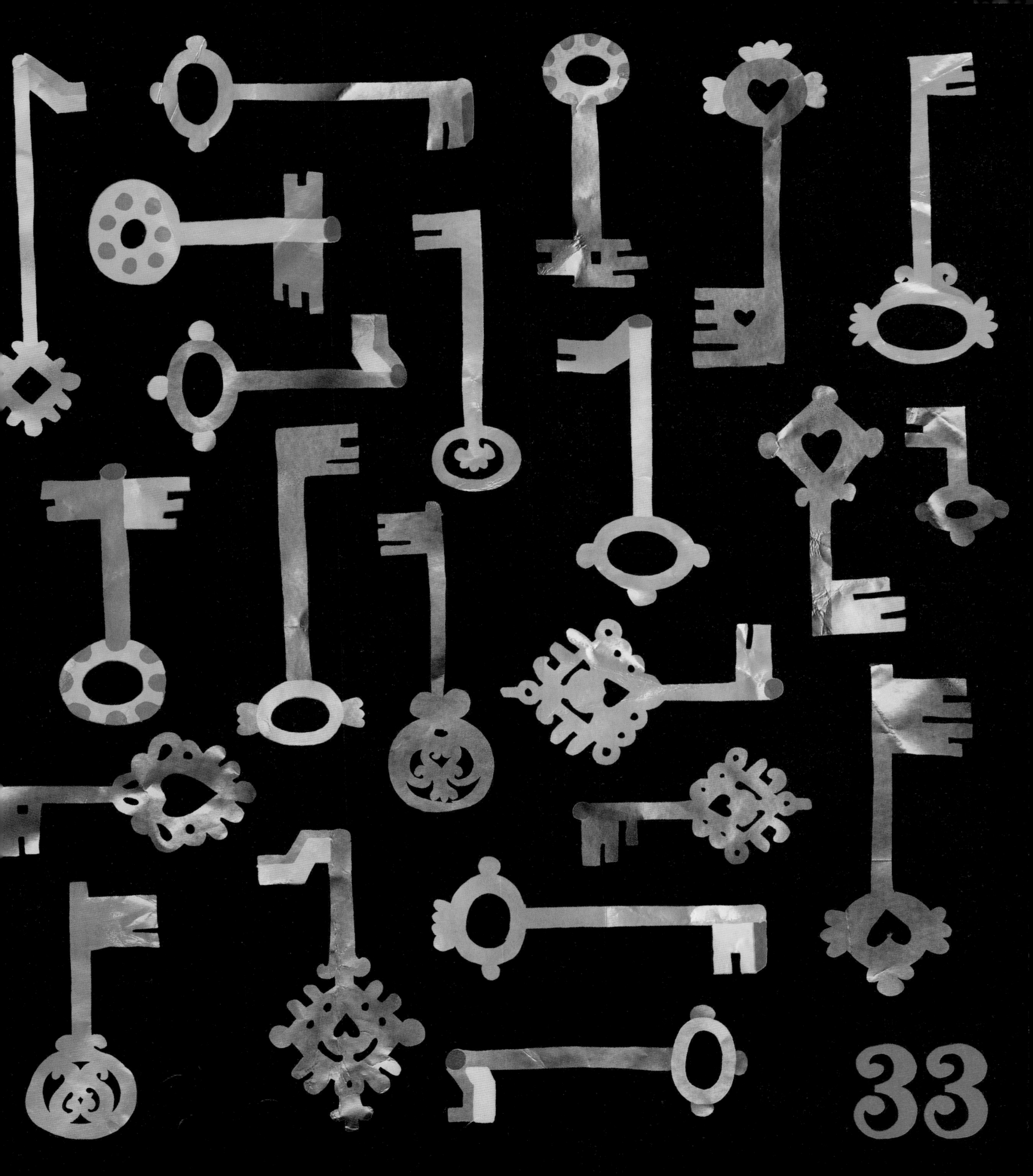
33

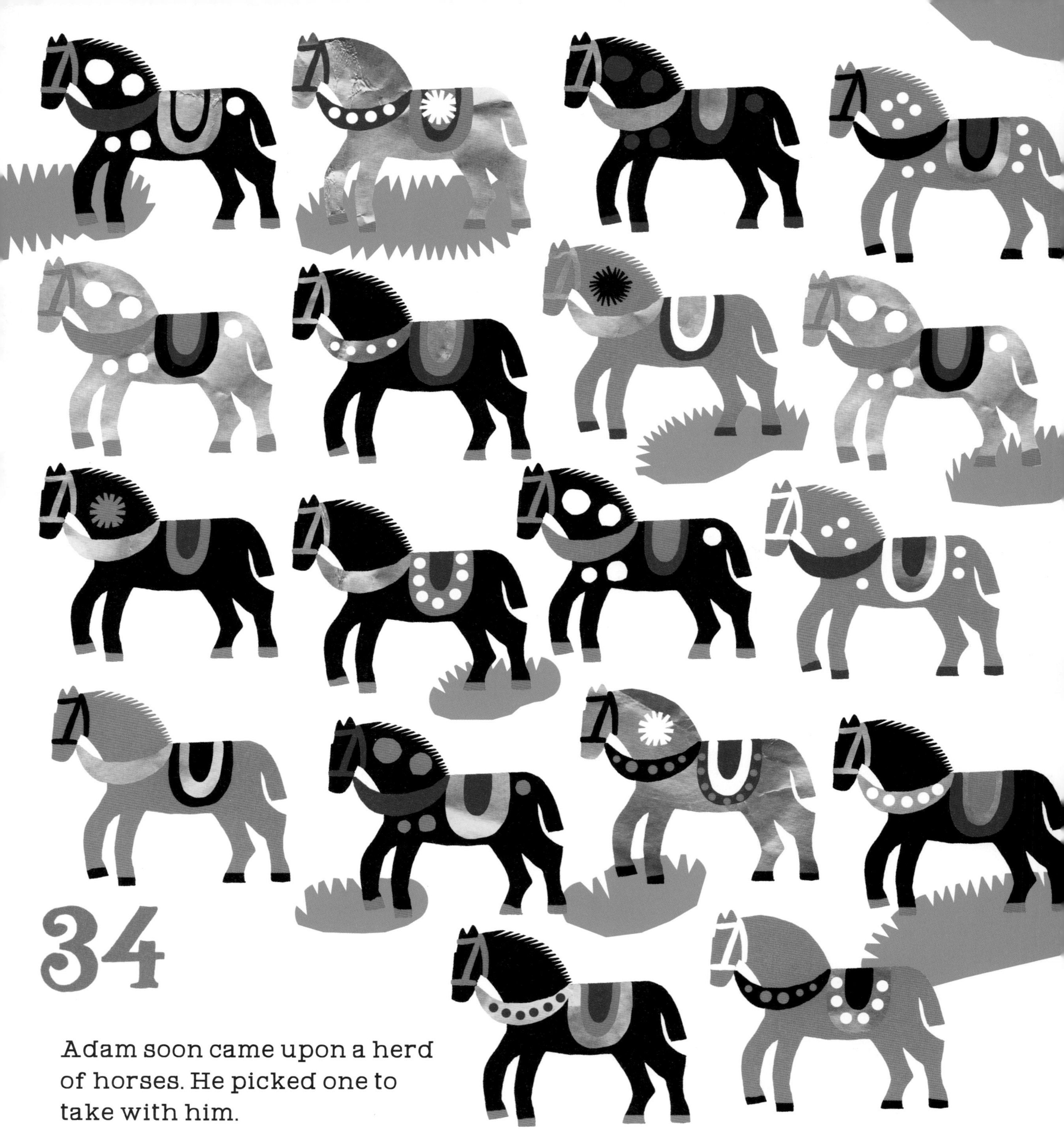

34

Adam soon came upon a herd of horses. He picked one to take with him.

*Find (and tame) the horse without a match.*

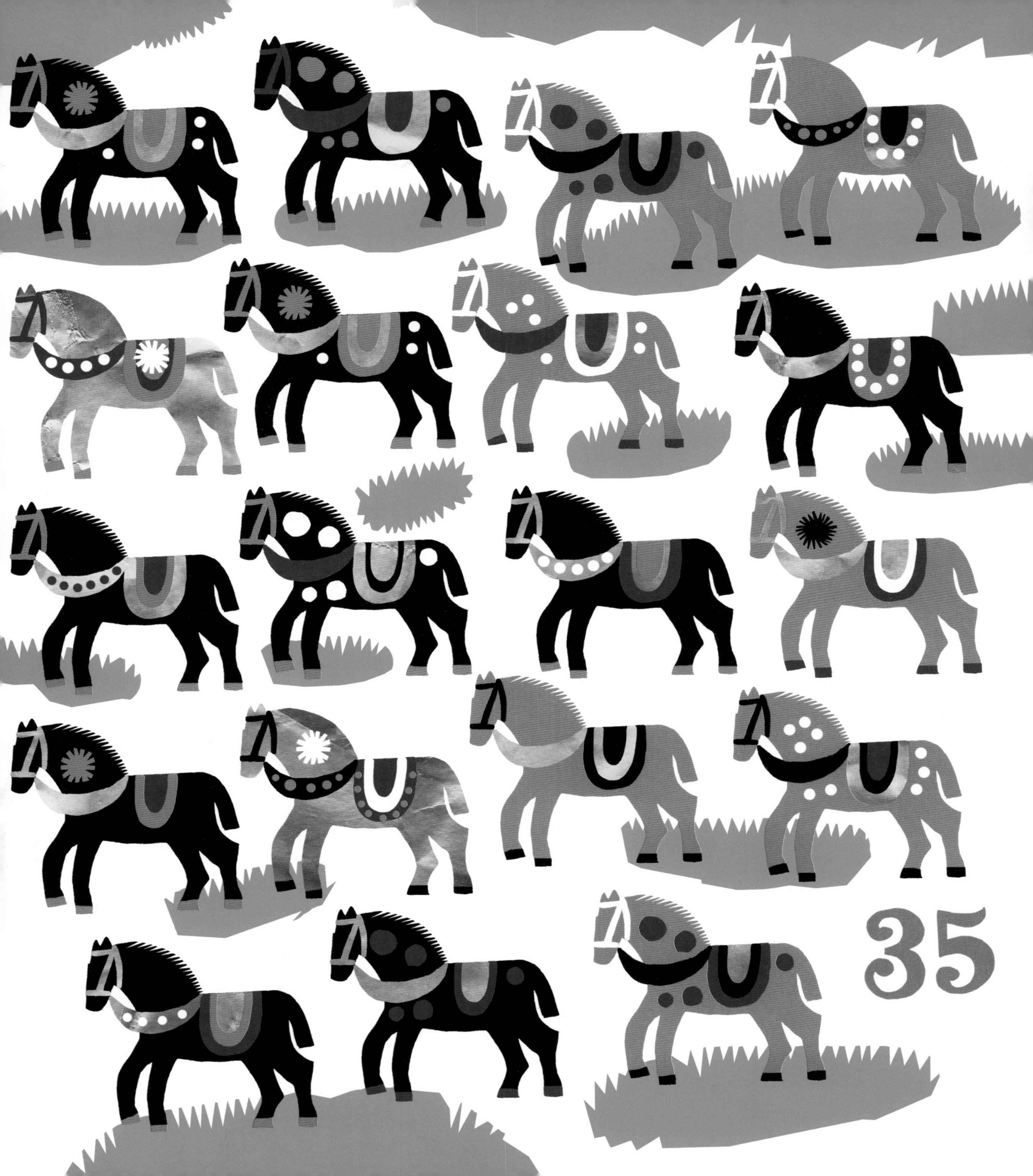
35

Next, Adam asked a fox for advice.

Find the way to the fox's den.
Share the piece of bread with him.

The fox sent Adam to the dwarves' house, in the darkest part of the forest.

*How many pairs of shoes do the dwarves have? How many hats? Is anything missing?*

40

The dwarves needed Adam's help to find their missing things. Adam asked others to help too.

*Ask the wisest fish, the one that looks different than the others.*

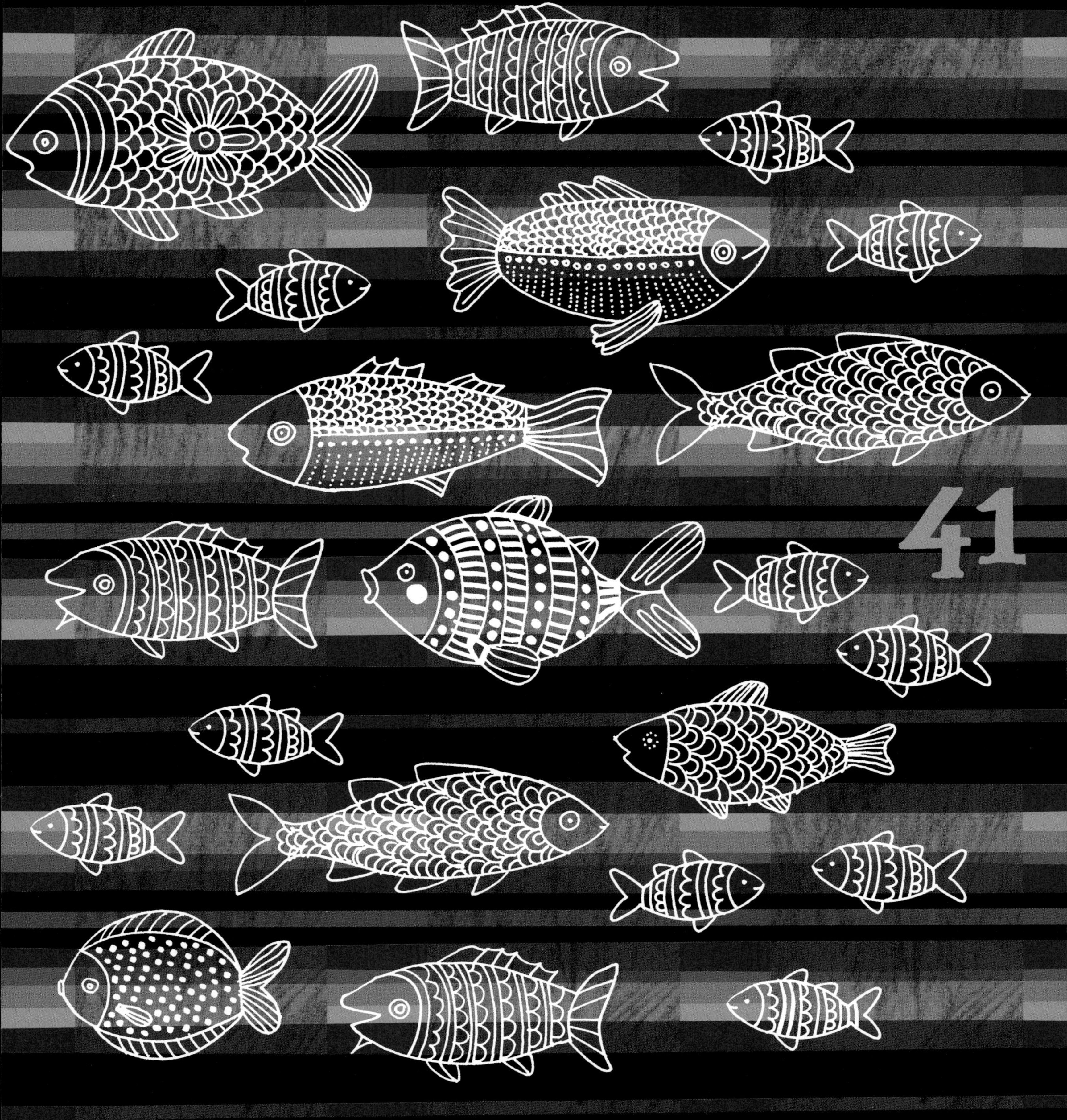
41

42

The wise fish told Adam
to search the fields.

*Spot the dwarves' missing shoe and hat.*

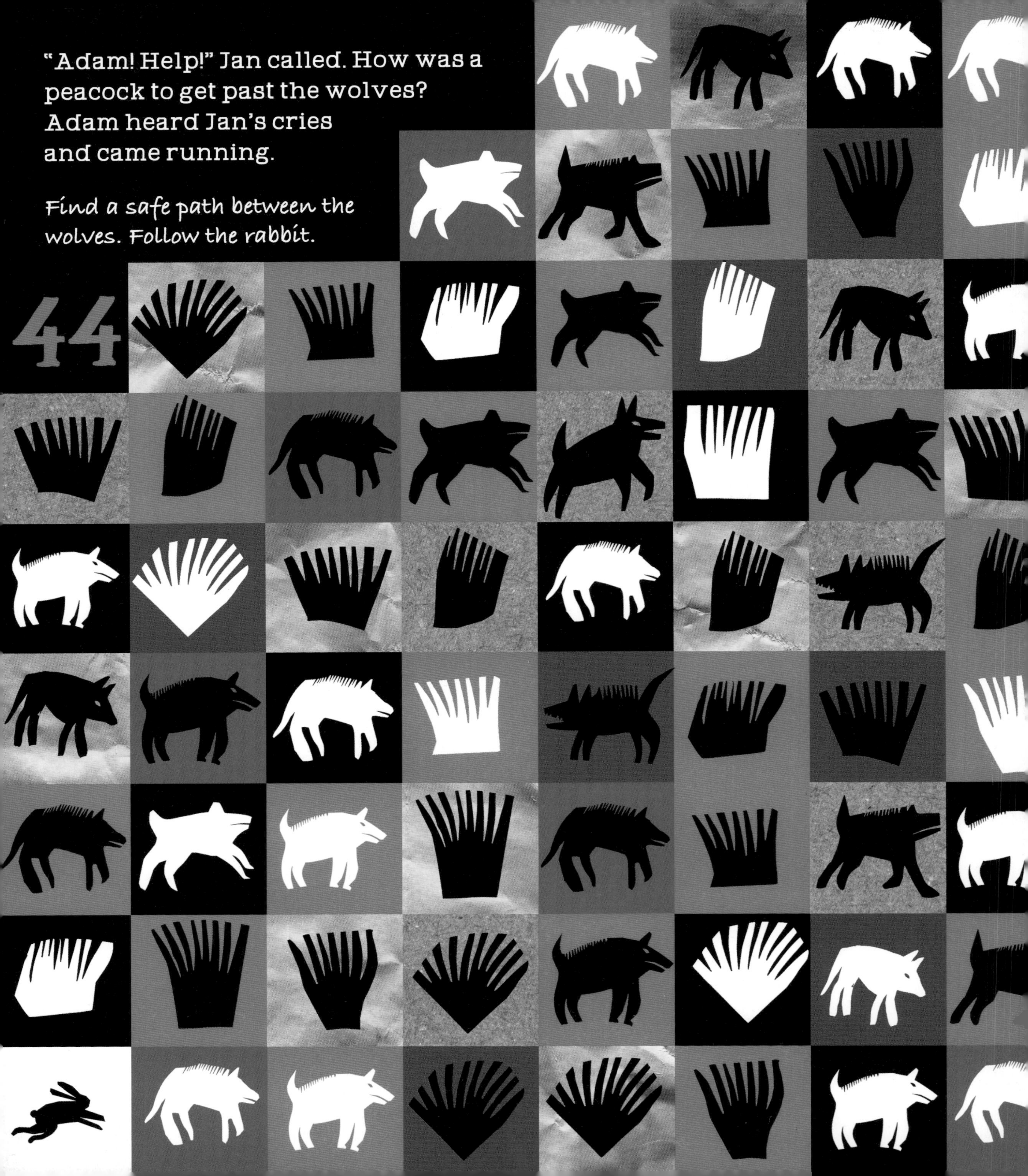
"Adam! Help!" Jan called. How was a peacock to get past the wolves? Adam heard Jan's cries and came running.
Find a safe path between the wolves. Follow the rabbit.
44

Adam and Jan escaped the woods.
But someone stole Jan's magic ring!

Which maiden has it? (Check page 12 to remember what it looks like.)

47

Adam found the thief, but she demanded a golden apple in exchange for the ring.

Find the way to the golden apple.

The thief took the golden apple . . .
then threw the magic ring into a
nearby pond.

Adam asked a lonely swan
to dive for the ring.

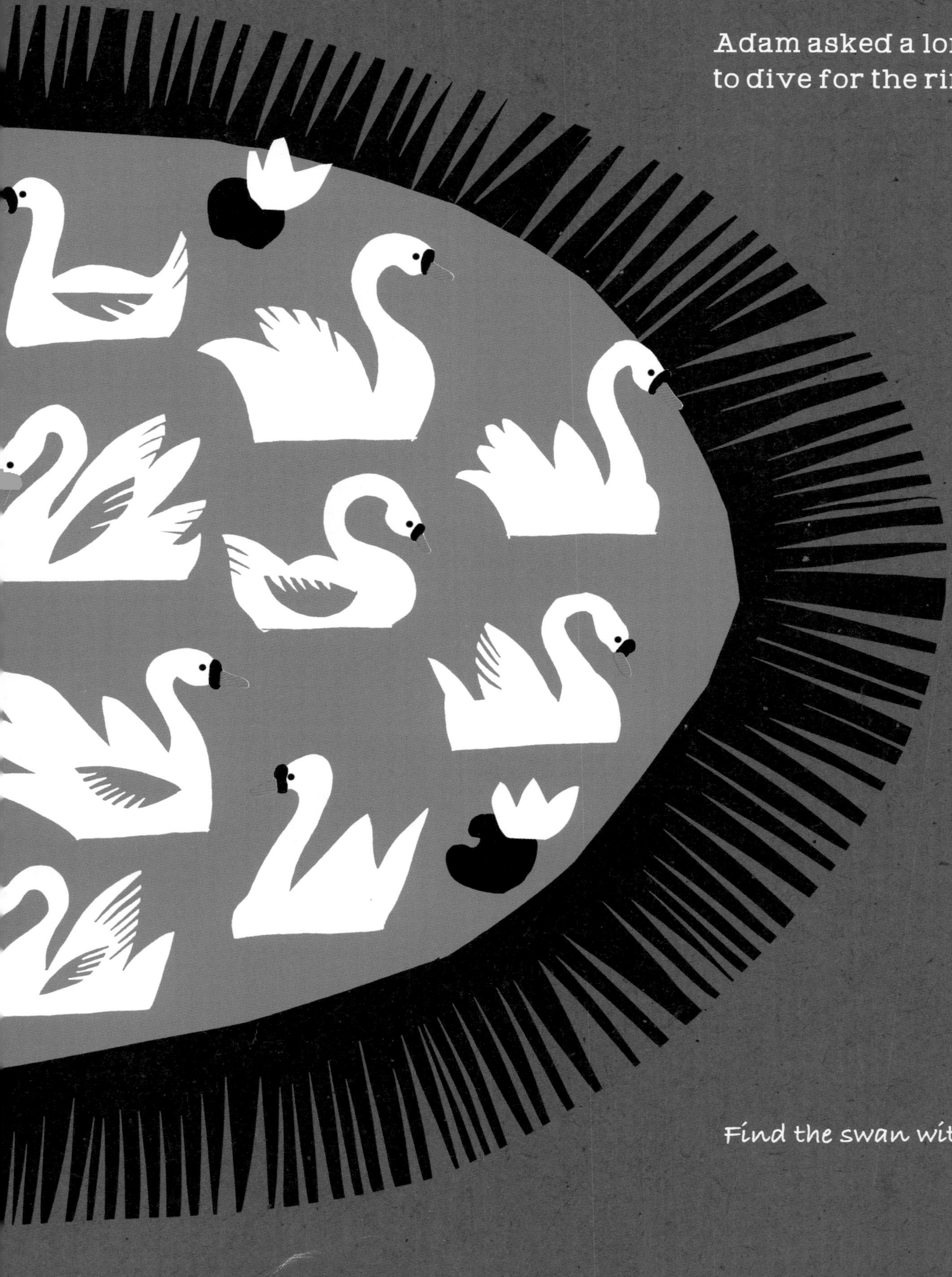

*Find the swan without a match.*

Adam took out his gold key, and they used Jan's ring to find the right door.



Which is the right door?

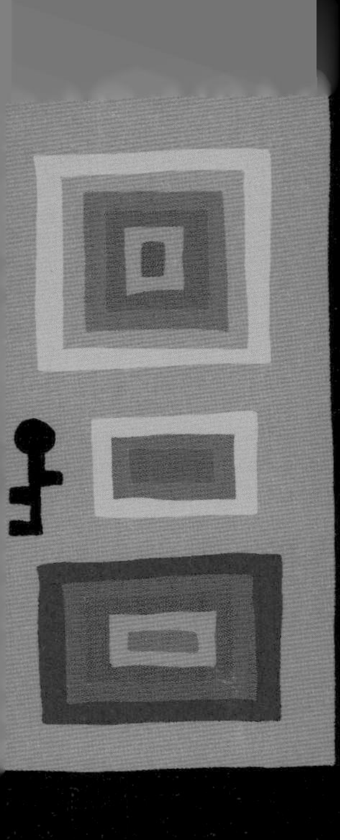

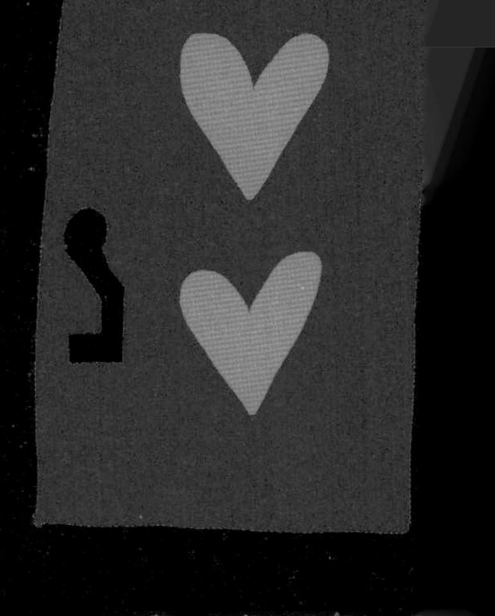

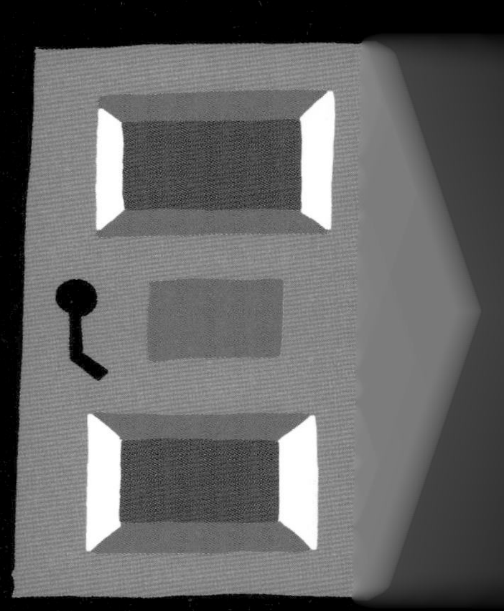

54

All at once . . .
treasure!
A voice came from nowhere:
"Take as much as you can carry, but beware. If you share with anyone, it will disappear."

*Find two identical jewels.*

BANG!

The gold crumbled into dirt,
and the jewels turned into toads.
(Brothers always share.)

*Find the five-fingered toad.*
*It's really a witch.*

*Find the six-fingered toad.*
*It's really an ogre.*

58

Dangerous creatures must be locked away!

*Find the way to the darkest part of the dungeon, then find the way out again.*

59

The gold and jewels were gone, but the spells were broken, the brothers were together and they were home.



Spot 10 differences between brothers.

The new friends they had made came from all over to celebrate.

The deer brought honey, the fox brought bread, and the dwarves brought vegetables and seeds.

The rabbit brought wood for the fire, and the doves made repairs while the horse trimmed the grass.

The fairies from the house at the end of the path brought a goat and fruit trees.

Adam and Jan didn't find their fortunes, but they were rich.

62
Can you
spot the dwarf
wearing the hat Adam
was searching for?

Together,
we can do
anything!

First American Edition 2018
Kane Miller, A Division of EDC Publishing



First published in Poland in 2017 by Egmont Polska.
This edition published under license from Egmont UK Ltd., The Yellow Building, 1 Nicholas Road, London W11 4AN



For information contact:
Kane Miller, A Division of EDC Publishing
PO Box 470663
Tulsa, OK 74147-0663
**www.kanemiller.com**
**www.usbornebooksandmore.com**
**www.edcpub.com**

Library of Congress Control Number: 2017942429

Printed in UE
2 3 4 5 6 7 8 9 10

ISBN: 978-1-61067-736-3

THE END